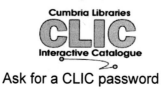

To the real Maia, Ionie, Harriet and Elissa,
whose beautiful names I have used – LC

To Mike – LF

STRIPES PUBLISHING
An imprint of the Little Tiger Group
1 Coda Studios, 189 Munster Road,
London SW6 6AW

A paperback original
First published in Great Britain in 2017

ISBN: 978-1-84715-790-4

Printed and bound in the UK.

2 4 6 8 10 9 7 5 3 1

Star Friends
Wish Trap

LINDA CHAPMAN
ILLUSTRATED BY LUCY FLEMING

IN THE STAR WORLD

The meadows and mountains, hills and valleys all glittered with sparkling stardust. The animals who lived in the Star World were going about their business but one snowy owl – Hunter – was watching something very important. In a pool, under a waterfall of stars, he could see what was happening in the human world.

He hooted softly: "Show me the Star Animals!" Peering curiously into the pool, he watched the images form, fade and re-form.

First he saw a fox cub curled up on a bed

beside a girl with dark-blond hair. His muzzle
was resting against her cheek and she was
stroking his fur. Next, a squirrel scampering
along the rail of a bunk bed, chattering to a
girl with black curls. Then he saw a gentle deer
being cuddled by a third girl with long dark
brown hair. In a fourth image, a wildcat was
weaving between the legs of a girl with red
hair and clever green eyes.

The owl nodded in satisfaction. Four of the young Star Animals who had recently made the journey from the Star World to the human world had found Star Friends. They would now teach those children how to use the magic that flowed between the Star World and the human world to do good deeds. Together the Star Animals and their new friends would try to stop anyone using dark magic to cause unhappiness and hurt people. They would help keep the human world safe.

As the owl watched, the image in the sparkling pool changed again, this time showing a person in a hooded cloak holding up a glittering black pendant above a small, squat shape. The owl stiffened and gave an anxious squawk as he watched shadows swirl about the shape. Dark magic was happening! There was no doubt about it – someone was about to cause trouble near to where the new Star Friends lived. Would the Star Friends and their animals realize? Would they be able to use their powers to stop the dark magic before people got hurt? He watched as the images continued to shift and change…

CHAPTER ONE

Maia Greene lay on her bed with Bracken the fox cub snoozing in her arms. Stroking his russet-red head, she felt her heart swell. It was hard to believe that she and Bracken had known each other for such a short time. But it was just two weeks and two days since she had seen him in the woods for the first time. Two weeks and two days since her life had changed forever.

Maia hugged Bracken closer. To start with she had thought he was just a young fox with unusual indigo eyes. But then he had spoken to

her and she had found out that he was a Star
Animal – a magical animal from a faraway place
called the Star World.

Bracken's eyes blinked open. Seeing her
gazing at him, he put his head on one side.
"What are you thinking about, Maia?"

"When you first told me you were a Star
Animal," Maia told him softly.

Bracken wriggled into a sitting position. "You
should have seen your face when I first spoke to
you," he teased. "You looked really shocked."

"Of course I did. It was the first time anything magical had ever happened to me," said Maia.

Bracken licked her nose. "And now you're my Star Friend and know all about magic."

Maia nodded. It was amazing and she could still hardly believe it. Every Star Animal who came to the human world had to find a child to be their Star Friend. Star Friends were able to hear and see the Star Animals because they believed in magic. Together they used the magic that flowed between the human world and the Star World to do good and to stop bad people who used dark magic to make others unhappy. Whenever Maia wanted Bracken, she could call his name and he would appear – but he was always careful to vanish when there were other people around.

Maia had been absolutely delighted when her best friends, Lottie and Sita, had also become Star Friends. Lottie's Star Animal was an energetic squirrel called Juniper and Sita's was a gentle deer called Willow. They were all having a brilliant – if sometimes scary – time learning about magic together.

Bracken jumped off the bed and shook himself. "Why don't you practise your magic? The more you practise, the better you'll get at it."

"OK," Maia said. Jumping up eagerly, she went to her desk with Bracken bounding around her legs. The desk's surface was covered with animal magazines, animal stickers, pens, pencils and books. Pushing them to one side, she leaned forwards, staring into her mirror.

One of the first things that Maia had learned when she started doing magic was that different Star Friends had different magical abilities. Her own magic was to do with sight. If she looked into a shiny surface, she could see things that were happening in other places. She could also see glimpses of the future and Bracken had told her that if she kept on practising she would be able to see into the past one day, too.

Focusing on the surface of the mirror, Maia let the rest of the world fade away and opened herself to the current of magic. It tingled through her body, making her feel like every centimetre of her skin was sparkling. What should she ask to see? She thought for a moment and then decided.

Show me the future. Show me something I need to see.

Her own reflection faded and a picture of a girl appeared in the mirror. She was crouched on the ground, hugging her ankle and crying. Maia frowned. The girl seemed to be wearing the red and grey uniform of Maia's school but Maia couldn't see her face. Who was she? What had happened to her?

I want to see more, Maia thought. But instead of the image becoming clearer, another image appeared. This time it was a different girl on a climbing frame. Maia couldn't see who it was but she was swinging from the top bar by her hands. As Maia watched, she lost her grip, cried out and fell.

Maia caught her breath as the girl hit the ground.

"What are you seeing?" Bracken asked curiously. Only Maia could see the images in the mirror.

"Two girls, in two separate images," Maia replied. "Both getting hurt. Wait, the image is changing again…"

Shock jolted through her as a new picture appeared – a skinny girl with shoulder-length black curly hair. She was staring at something that was coming towards her and she looked terrified.

"It's Lottie!" Maia exclaimed, recognizing her friend.

The image disappeared, leaving Maia looking at her own reflection, her wide green eyes staring back at her and her dark-blond fringe falling across her face. She swung round. "There was something coming towards Lottie and she looked really scared. Do you think she's OK?"

"Use your magic to find out," Bracken urged.

Maia turned back to the mirror. *I want to see Lottie wherever she is right now.*

A new image appeared in the glass – Lottie was in her bedroom, practising handstands, her black curls brushing the floor. To Maia's relief, she looked just fine. A red squirrel with a fluffy tail and bright, inquisitive eyes was scampering along the top of the bunk bed.

Maia's breath rushed out. "It's OK, she's with Juniper in her bedroom."

"What did you ask the magic to show you when you saw those images?" Bracken said.

"I asked it to show me something in the future that I needed to see."

Bracken looked troubled. "Then the magic will have shown you those things for a reason.

Maybe they're going to happen because of dark magic." His ears flattened.

Maia stared at him. "You mean, you think there might be another Shade nearby?"

Bracken nodded and Maia's heart beat a little faster. People who used dark magic could conjure horrible spirits called Shades from the shadows. The Shade would then either be set free to bring chaos and unhappiness wherever it went, or it could be trapped in an object and given to someone who the person doing dark magic wanted to harm.

Maia had already encountered one Shade, which had been trapped in a make-up compact. It had talked to Clio, her older sister, from within the little mirror, twisting her mind and making her feel jealous of her best friend. Thankfully Maia, Lottie and Sita had managed to defeat it and send it back to the shadows. But only with the help of another Star Friend, Ionie.

Bracken padded round anxiously. "I think you should talk to the others. If there is another Shade, we must try and stop it."

"You're right. I'll get them to meet me at the clearing." Maia picked up her phone and typed in Lottie and Sita's names. After a moment's hesitation, she added Ionie into the message, too.

She and Ionie used to be friends when they were younger but they didn't get on at all now. Still, like it or not, Ionie *was* a Star Friend and had helped send the last Shade back to the shadows. Maia had to include her. She tapped in her message.

Need 2 talk 2 u all. It's important. C u at clearing in 45 mins. Mx

She pressed send.

Chapter Two

Going downstairs, Maia heard Clio calling out to their mum. "I'm going to babysit Paige for a few hours, Mum. I'll be back at seven."

"OK," Mrs Greene said, coming to the kitchen door with Alfie, Maia's little brother. "Say hi to Paige's mum and dad for me."

"I will," said Clio.

"Train!" said Alfie, spotting his model train by the bottom of the stairs. Mrs Greene put him down and he toddled over to it.

Maia smiled at him. "Chooo-choo!"

She pushed it across the floor and he followed it, giggling in delight.

Maia unhooked her coat from the pegs by the door. "I'm going out, too, Mum. Is that OK?"

"Where are you off to?" her mum asked.

"To the woods to meet up with Lottie and Sita. Ionie might come, too." She'd already had texts back from Sita and Lottie saying they would meet her there but she hadn't heard from Ionie yet.

Her mum smiled. "So you and Ionie are friends again now?"

"Um … kind of," Maia said, wondering what her mum would say if she told her the truth – that she was only including Ionie because they were all Star Friends and could do magic.

Her mum looked pleased. "I've always liked Ionie. You were such good friends when you were little – always playing make-believe games about magic and animals. I'm glad you're becoming close again now you're in the same class at school."

At the start of the school year, the teachers had shuffled the classes around. Sita and Lottie had been put in one Year Six class while Maia was in the other. As if being separated from her best friends wasn't bad enough, she had also ended up sitting next to Ionie. Ionie was really clever but she was impatient and seemed to love pointing out any mistakes that

Maia made. Ionie didn't have many friends in the class and spent most of her lunchtimes reading.

"Why don't you have a sleepover next weekend and invite Ionie, Sita and Lottie?" Mrs Greene went on. "You could have a bonfire in the garden and toast marshmallows."

Maia wasn't sure that was a good idea – Lottie found Ionie even more annoying than she did! But her mum was looking at her expectantly. "OK, thanks, Mum. I'll ask the others," she agreed. "Bye, Mum. Bye, Alfie."

"Chooo-choo!" said Alfie, waving his train at her.

Maia shut the door behind her and did up the zip on her coat. Although the autumn sun was shining, there was little warmth in its rays and the wind was blowing fallen leaves into piles.

As she wheeled her bike out from the garage, Maia caught sight of Clio heading down the street just ahead. Maia cycled to catch up with her.

"Oh, hi," said Clio as Maia jumped off her bike. "Where are you off to?"

"The woods by Granny Anne's cottage," said Maia.

"Again?" said Clio in surprise. "Why don't you all meet at home where it's warm?" She shivered and dug her hands into the pockets of her coat.

"We like it there." Maia wished she could tell Clio it was because of the Star Animals – it was where they had first appeared and it was a particularly good place to do magic. It was private and overgrown and hardly anyone ever went there.

"Doesn't it make you feel sad – going past Granny Anne's cottage all the time?" Clio said curiously.

"Only a little bit," said Maia. Their granny had died just over a month ago. At first Maia hadn't liked going near the cottage at all. But since she'd found out about the Star Animals, she'd started to feel differently. She suspected her granny had been a Star Friend, too. Granny Anne had always told Maia to believe in magic, and she had been very kind and helped lots of people in the village. Thinking that she might have been a Star Friend helped Maia feel close to her still.

Clio sighed. "I really miss Granny Anne.

Paige does, too. She was talking about her last time I babysat. I think it's harder for her – she's only seven." Paige was Granny Anne's goddaughter and had been very close to her.

"Look, there's Paige," Maia said, pointing down the street.

Paige was bouncing on a trampoline in the front garden, turning effortless somersaults. Spotting them, she waved, and by the time they reached the driveway, she had scrambled off the trampoline.

"Hi." She grinned. Her brown hair was tied in two bunches and she had a smattering of freckles across her nose.

"Hi, Paige. I'll just go and tell your mum I'm here," said Clio.

"Are you going to play with me, Maia?" Paige asked as Clio headed into the house.

"Sorry, Paige, I can't stop today. I'm going to see my friends," said Maia.

"Are you seeing Lottie?" asked Paige eagerly. She and Lottie went to the same gymnastics club, and Maia knew Paige really admired her.

She nodded. "I am."

"Say hi to her for me!" Paige said.

"Maia!"

Maia looked round. "You can say hi yourself," she said with a smile as she saw Lottie and Sita cycling down the street towards them.

"Lottie!" Paige squealed in excitement.

Lottie and Sita got off their bikes, and Paige ran to give Lottie a hug.

"Hi, Paige," said Lottie.

"Do you want to see how good my backwards walkover is getting?" said Paige. Without waiting for a reply, she put her arms over her head and dropped back into a bridge. "What do you think?" she said, the ends of her brown bunches dangling down.

"That's really good, Paige," said Lottie.

"I've been practising every day," said Paige proudly as she flipped back to her feet. "I really, really want to be in the gym display team like you. I want it *so* much!"

"Keep on practising and I bet you will be," said Lottie. "You're already third reserve."

Paige looked hopefully at her. "Do you want to have a go on the trampoline – we can practise somersaults?"

"We really should get going," said Maia, catching Lottie's eye. As she turned to leave, she noticed a pottery gnome tucked beside a nearby shrub. He was about as tall as her knees and had a little red hat, a green waistcoat and the words "Make a Wish" on his brown belt.

"That's a cute gnome," Maia said.

Paige patted his head. "One of Mum's friends gave him to us at the weekend. Mum's been trying to decide where to put him. I like him here by the trampoline. I've told him I really wish I get on the gym team!"

"I hope your wish comes true!" Lottie said, smiling at her.

They said goodbye and headed off. As they cycled towards the clearing, Maia told them about the bonfire sleepover her mum had suggested.

"That sounds fun!" said Sita.

"There's only one catch," Maia said. "Mum wants me to invite Ionie, too."

Lottie's face fell. "Do we have to?"

"Oh, Lottie, don't be mean," said Sita. "When we practised magic together on Wednesday after school, she was fine."

"You mean apart from saying she was surprised Maia couldn't see into the past properly yet. Oh, and telling me that she was glad she didn't have agility as her magic skill because doing stealth magic and being able to shadow-travel was much cooler."

Sita frowned. "She didn't *exactly* say that. She just said she wouldn't want to run and jump and climb like you do. And when she was talking to Maia, I think she wanted to see if she could help."

"Maia doesn't need her help," said Lottie. "She's brilliant at doing her magic."

Maia shot her friend a grateful look. It was

lovely that Lottie was so loyal, even if Ionie was right about the fact that she hadn't managed to see into the past.

"I don't think Ionie means to be annoying," Sita said. "I think she wants to be friends and she's trying to get us to like her. She just doesn't always go about it in the right way."

"You can say that again," Lottie muttered. She caught Sita's eye and sighed. "OK. I won't be mean and I'll give her a chance. But I'd much rather it was just us – and I don't like that cat of hers at all."

Lottie was talking about Ionie's Star Animal, a very smug wildcat called Sorrel.

"I know what you mean," Maia said. "I don't particularly want to invite Ionie but Mum really wants me to." She pushed the problem to the back of her mind. "I'll decide later. Right now, we've got other stuff to talk about."

"What sort of stuff?" said Lottie.

"Important magic stuff!" said Maia. "Come on!"

Putting their heads down, they cycled as fast as they could to the clearing.

CHAPTER THREE

The village where Maia and her friends lived
was called Westcombe, on the North Devon
coast. Most of the village was on one side
of the main road, set back in a maze of little
streets. On the other side of the road were a
few houses, as well as the woods that led to the
clifftops, the shingle beach and the sea.

Maia, Lottie and Sita crossed the main road
carefully and pushed their bikes on to a narrow
stony lane with woods on both sides. Overhead,
seagulls were circling in the grey sky. At the top

of the lane was a row of little houses with neat front gardens. Further down was Granny Anne's thatched cottage and beyond that, the track led on down to the clifftop and the beach.

Maia glanced at the row of stone houses at the top of the lane. Ionie lived in the end one with her mum and dad. Maia thought about cycling straight past but then she felt a pang of guilt. "Should we see if Ionie's in? She might not have got my text."

Maia noticed there was no car in the driveway. Pulling out her phone, she checked it and saw that a message had just come through from Ionie:

Out at my grandma's. Will come and meet you as soon as I get back. Ix

Maia hurried back to the others, feeling secretly relieved it would just be the three of them and their Star Animals for a while. "She's sent me a text – she's not in but she says she'll meet us later."

They cycled on down the lane, bumping over the potholes and trying not to skid on fallen leaves.

Leaving their bikes in Granny Anne's garden, they pushed their way along the overgrown footpath that led to the clearing in the woods. Hearing the sound of the stream splashing up ahead, Maia's heart quickened in excitement. She sped up and burst into the clearing with Sita and Lottie at her heels. Instantly Bracken the fox, Juniper the squirrel and Willow the deer appeared. Bracken spun in circles, yapping, Willow cantered straight over to Sita, pricking her ears in delight, while Juniper scampered up a nearby tree trunk and leaped from branch to branch.

"Race me, Lottie!" Juniper chattered.

In a flash, Lottie was scrambling up the tree after him. She was brilliant at gymnastics anyway but when she drew on the current of Star Magic she could run and jump and throw with amazing speed and skill. She whooped as she swung after Juniper, as agile as a squirrel herself.

Willow nuzzled Sita's hands while Bracken raced round Maia and stopped in a play bow, his bottom in the air and his tail waving. "I love being here!" he said.

Maia laughed. She knew she had to tell the others about what she'd seen in the mirror but for a moment she just wanted to enjoy herself. "Me, too."

Lottie grabbed a hazelnut from a bush and threw it gently at Maia. Her accuracy was spot on and it hit Maia's head. "Just getting some target practice in!" she said, grinning cheekily.

She somersaulted effortlessly down to the ground but too late she realized that she had landed in a pile of nettles. "Ow!" she yelped.

"Don't worry," Sita called. "I'll help."

Lottie hobbled over and Sita laid her hands on the nettle stings. Within a few seconds the pain had cleared from Lottie's face.

"You've made it better," Lottie said, examining her leg. The rash had vanished.

Sita grinned. She was still amazed by the way her healing abilities worked. "It's just like magic!"

Lottie chuckled and then ran towards Maia. "Tag!" she said, tapping Maia's shoulder and darting away.

Maia raced after her. She couldn't begin to match Lottie's speed but she could use her magic to see where Lottie was heading. It was a strange feeling. When the magic was flowing through her, she just had to relax until she saw a shining outline appear around Lottie. The outline moved a split second before Lottie did, which meant Maia could sprint to the right place. "Got you!" she cried in triumph as her outstretched fingers touched Lottie's shoulder.

Lottie tagged her back in an instant and climbed a tree trunk.

"No going up trees!" called Sita who was watching with her arm round Willow's neck. "That's not fair on Maia."

Lottie leaped down and raced to the river, leaping sure-footedly from one slippery rock to another. "Can't catch me, Maia!"

"Someone's coming!" called Sita in alarm.

In an instant the three Star Animals vanished. Lottie and Maia swung round, just as a girl with red hair came pushing through the cow parsley into the clearing.

Ionie, Maia realized with relief.

A wildcat with a sleek tabby coat and slanting indigo eyes materialized at Ionie's side. Bracken, Juniper and Willow instantly reappeared, too.

"Sorry we're late," Ionie said.

"Don't worry," said Sita, smiling. "We haven't done anything yet really."

Sorrel, the wildcat, stalked forwards. "I can see that. I would have thought you would have been practising your magic *properly*."

"Just because the girls were having fun, doesn't mean they weren't learning more about their magic," Bracken protested. "They're … um…"

"Practising teamwork," Juniper put in helpfully.

"That's it, practising teamwork!" said Bracken.

"Hmm," Sorrel said disbelievingly. Sitting down, she flicked her tail round her paws. "Well, now Ionie and I are here, why doesn't Ionie show you all how well she can shadow-travel. Ionie's magical abilities are coming on in leaps and bounds," she said smugly.

"Should I show you what I can do now?" Ionie said eagerly, walking to a patch of shadows under an oak tree and looking at the others. "I've learned to use shadows to travel wherever I want. I just imagine where I want to go and then I come out in the nearest patch of shadows to that place. Watch!" She stepped into the shadows and disappeared, appearing a few seconds later in another patch of shadows on the far side of the clearing. "Ta-da!" she said, grinning and holding up her hands. "Isn't that awesome?"

"That's great!" said Sita, clapping.

"Exceptional girl," purred Sorrel. "So talented."

Lottie rolled her eyes at Maia.

"What?" Ionie said in surprise, catching the look. "Don't you two think it's good?"

"Yeah," said Maia, shrugging. "It's great, I guess." It *was* a cool thing to do but did Ionie really have to show off quite so much?

"I'll do it again," Ionie said quickly, as if afraid she wasn't impressing them enough. "I'll go further this time."

Bracken nudged Maia's hand. "Maia, you

need to tell the others what you saw in the mirror earlier."

"Oh yes," Maia remembered. "Wait, Ionie! There's something I really have to talk to everyone about. I saw some things when I was using my magic at home earlier – worrying things."

"Yes, let's listen to Maia," said Lottie, giving Ionie a pointed look. "After all, that's why we came here. Not to watch you do magic."

Ionie frowned. "I only wanted to show you because I think it's really important that we know each other's abilities – especially if we have to fight a Shade again one day."

"Ionie's right," said Sita. "It is important, so we can work as a team. But right now, why don't we hear what Maia has to say? Let's sit down and she can tell us what's going on."

As she listened to Sita's words, Maia felt her irritation melt away and she found herself nodding in agreement. Sita's magic meant she was able to calm and soothe people and animals as well as healing them, and she was getting better at it all the time.

The tension vanished and they all sat down on rocks and tree stumps. Maia quickly told them about the images she'd seen in the mirror. "The third image was of a girl with something coming towards her," she finished. She decided not to mention that it was Lottie, in case it worried her friend. "She looked really scared."

"I wonder why you saw those things?" said Sita.

"Maia asked the magic to show her what she needed to see," Bracken explained. "It must have shown her those images because they're important in some way in the future."

"Maybe, maybe not," Sorrel said with a shrug. "Everyone knows that looking into the future is a particularly difficult type of magic. Maia might just have got it wrong."

"I bet she didn't!" Lottie protested.

Willow jumped in quickly. "What do you think we should do, Bracken?"

"I think we should investigate," he said. "I'm worried that Maia saw those images because a Shade will make those things happen."

"Do we have to look out for creepy talking mirrors again?" said Sita with a shiver.

Willow shook her head. "The Shade could be trapped in any object."

"The deer is right," said Sorrel. "There are all different kinds of Shades – Nightmare Shades, Ink Shades, Wish Shades. Some live in mirrors and talk to people and make them do bad things, like that Mirror Shade. Others can bring bad luck or trap people in different ways."

"Are Shades controlled by the person who conjured them?" Ionie asked.

"No," said Sorrel. "A Shade can be trapped but not controlled. Someone using dark magic can choose which type of Shade best suits their evil purposes. Then they trap them in an object and put it in someone's possession. If a Shade is not trapped, they will be free to affect whoever they like."

"But who would trap a Shade – and why?" said Sita.

"Someone who wanted to cause trouble," said Sorrel darkly.

"What should we do?" said Lottie.

"Well, if you all really think we need to

take these visions seriously, we should try and find out if any dark magic has been used," said Sorrel. "As you all know, I am excellent at smelling out Shades."

"Willow can smell out Shades, too," Lottie pointed out.

"Not as well as Sorrel," admitted Willow.

Just as humans had different abilities with magic, Star Animals also had different abilities and some of them were more sensitive to dark magic than others.

"I know, Sorrel! Why don't you and I shadow-travel around to see if you can detect a Shade anywhere in the village?" Ionie suggested.

Maia nodded in agreement. "Good plan."

Ionie jumped to her feet.

"Wait!" said Lottie quickly. "That's too dangerous. What if you do find a Shade and get into a fight with it?"

"There won't be a fight," said Ionie. "I'm a Spirit Speaker, remember. If I meet a Shade

I can just command it to go back to the shadows."

Sorrel rubbed her head against Ionie's hand. "Your bravery is admirable, Ionie. But it may not be that simple. Remember what I have told you – you need a Shade to look you in the eyes before you can command it, and you need to be in full control of your magic."

"Don't go off on your own, Ionie," said Sita. "The Mirror Shade was horrible."

"Sita's right," said Lottie. "I think we should wait and see what happens. If there is a Shade nearby then strange things will start to happen. When they do, we can come up with a plan."

"No! I think we should try and stop bad things *before* they happen. We should do something right now." Ionie turned impatiently to Maia. "Maia, you agree with me, don't you?"

Maia remembered the image she had seen of Lottie looking terrified. She desperately wanted to stop that from happening but she didn't think Ionie should really go rushing off on her own, and she also didn't want to hurt Lottie and Sita's feelings by siding with Ionie. Perhaps Sorrel was right and the images she had seen weren't going to come true. "Umm…" She glanced round. "Well, maybe we don't need to do anything just yet."

Ionie frowned. "You don't really think that."

"Yes, she does," said Lottie, linking arms with Maia. "And Sita agrees with us, too. Don't you, Sita?"

Sita gave a nod.

Sorrel glared at Bracken. "Come on, fox. You know we need to act. Persuade your human to change her mind."

Bracken pressed against Maia's legs. "Whatever Maia wants, I'm happy with."

"It's decided then," said Lottie quickly. "If a Shade is doing things, it will become obvious and we can make a plan then. In the meantime, we just wait."

Ionie's mouth tightened as she looked at the three of them standing together. "Fine. I'm going home."

"Ionie – don't," said Sita, holding out her hand.

But Ionie ignored her. She walked towards a shadow at the edge of the clearing and Sorrel leaped after her. As soon as Ionie's feet touched the shadow, she vanished. Sorrel hissed at the others and then vanished, too.

"Oh, why does Ionie have to be a Star

Friend?" Lottie cried in frustration.

"We shouldn't have upset her," said Sita.

"All we did was vote against her plan," said Lottie. "There was no need for her to go off in a big huff."

Maia felt torn. She couldn't stop thinking about the image of Lottie and wondering if she should have sided with Ionie. What if the things she had seen *were* accurate and something horrible happened to her friend? What if it turned out she could have done something to stop it? An icy finger ran down her spine.

Juniper leaped from Lottie's shoulders, ran to a nearby tree and raced up the trunk. "Let's not just stand around. We should make the most of the time that's left."

"Juniper's right," said Lottie. "Let's practise our magic. If we do end up fighting a Shade again, we'll need our magic to be as strong as possible. The more we practise the better we'll get."

She charged after Juniper and climbed the

tree. She swung on to a high branch and dropped down, so she was dangling from her hands, then she swung along the branch like a monkey.

Sita went to the base of the tree and repaired the stems of a clump of ferns that had been squashed in the earlier game of tag.

Bracken nudged Maia's hand with his nose. "Are you going to practise your magic, too?"

She sighed. "I don't really feel like it." Kneeling down, she wrapped her arms round him and hugged him tight. He licked her cheek comfortingly.

Oh, please let Lottie be OK, Maia thought as she watched Lottie drop down from the branch and cartwheel effortlessly across the grass. *Please let the vision I saw be wrong.*

Chapter Four

When the sun started to set, the girls went to
fetch their bikes from Granny Anne's garden.
A slim, grey-haired lady was pruning the rose
bush beside the front door.

"Auntie Mabel!" Maia said, waving.

The old lady looked round. "Hello, Maia.
I thought I'd pop down here and tidy up the
garden for your mum and dad."

"That's really kind of you," Maia said. Auntie
Mabel had been one of Granny Anne's closest
friends.

Lottie and Sita picked up their bikes. "You two go on," Maia told them. "I'll stay with Auntie Mabel for a while."

"OK. See you tomorrow," Sita said, and she and Lottie cycled away up the lane.

"So, how are you?" Auntie Mabel asked Maia.

"Good, thanks. How about you, Auntie Mabel?"

"Oh, I've been keeping myself busy," Auntie Mabel replied. "I'm helping with the Bonfire Night event in the playing field next week. I've also been tidying up the village green and doing some knitting for the Christmas Fayre."

"Granny Anne used to do all those things," Maia said, feeling a flicker of sadness.

"I know," Auntie Mabel said. "I've never really got involved before but now she's no longer with us, I thought I should step in and help. I have to say, I'm quite enjoying it." Clipping her pruning shears shut, she sat down on a bench at the front of the cottage. She patted it and Maia sat down beside her. "When I saw you a few weeks ago, you told me about a young fox with indigo eyes that you'd seen in the woods. Have you seen him again?"

Maia hesitated. The Star Animals were a secret but surely it was OK to say she'd seen him again. "Actually, I have. Quite a few times."

"And…" the old lady prompted.

"And what?" said Maia, puzzled.

Auntie Mabel dropped her voice. "Have you discovered his secret?"

Maia stared. *Secret?* Auntie Mabel couldn't know about Star Animals, could she? Bracken had said there weren't any other Star Animals in the area, so she knew Auntie Mabel couldn't be a Star Friend.

Auntie Mabel leaned even closer. "Have you discovered that he's a Star Animal, Maia?"

Maia's mouth fell open in surprise.

Auntie Mabel chuckled as she saw the shock on her face. "It's all right, my dear. I know all about Star Animals – your granny was a Star Friend. Did you know that?"

"No … but … but I thought she might have been," stammered Maia. "Are you a Star Friend, too?"

Auntie Mabel shook her head. "I always wanted to be but I was never lucky enough to meet a Star Animal. Once when we were about the same age as you, I turned up at your granny's house unexpectedly and saw her with her Star Animal – she was a silver wolf."

Mia caught her breath. A silver wolf! Granny Anne had always loved wolves – her cottage had been full of wolf pictures and ornaments. That explained why!

"Your granny explained to me about Star Animals and swore me to secrecy," Auntie Mabel went on. "She would tell me about her magic adventures and, when I got a bit older, I learned that you didn't need to be a Star Friend to do magic. I found out how to use crystals to channel magic to heal and help people." She patted Maia's hand. "Your granny and I worked together over the years. Now you're a Star Friend, I'd like to do the same with you, too."

Maia was lost for words. Part of her was really excited at the thought of talking to Auntie Mabel about magic. But she had promised Bracken she wouldn't mention the Star World to anyone who wasn't a Star Friend. She hesitated. If Auntie Mabel knew about it already and if Granny Anne had trusted her, then surely it would be fine if she did, too?

"Would you like my help?" Auntie Mabel's eyes twinkled.

Maia smiled. "Yes, please!"

"So the fox is your Star Animal?" said Auntie Mabel.

"He's called Bracken," Maia said. "Lottie, Sita and Ionie are Star Friends, too."

"You lucky, lucky girls," said Auntie Mabel. "Have you learned about your magical abilities yet?"

Maia nodded. "My abilities are to do with sight."

"Interesting," said Auntie Mabel thoughtfully. "Your granny's abilities were to do with healing. Are you finding it easy to use your magic?"

"Sort of," said Maia. "Although I'm no good at seeing the past yet. I have seen some things from the future but I'm not sure if they're accurate."

"Very few people see the future clearly when they first start using magic," said Auntie Mabel.

Maia felt relieved. It would be much better if the things she'd seen weren't really going to happen.

"If you want to improve, you need to try really hard," Auntie Mabel advised. "You have to concentrate on forcing the magic to work for you. That's what works for me when I do magic."

Maia frowned. "But Bracken told me not to try and force the magic. He said it would work better if I relax."

"That's only at first," said Auntie Mabel. "When you get used to doing it, you have to really focus on what you want to achieve."

"Oh, OK," said Maia. "Thank you."

Auntie Mable patted her hand. "Do you know much about dark magic yet?" she asked.

"We had to fight a Shade last week." Maia explained about the Shade in the mirror.

"And now Bracken thinks there might be another Shade nearby because I saw some horrible things happening when I asked the magic to show me the future."

"Oh, my dear. Please don't worry too much. Your visions probably aren't accurate at the moment." Auntie Mabel gave Maia a kindly smile. "I can't tell you how many times I got things wrong when I first started seeing into the future. It would be really unusual to have to face another Shade so soon unless someone was conjuring them up from the Shadows on purpose. But I'm sure that's not happening in Westcombe. Look, to put your mind at rest, how about I use my crystals to check? I'll soon find out if there's anything strange going on."

"That would be great. Thank you!" Maia felt as if a weight had dropped from her shoulders. If Auntie Mabel could check to see if there was a Shade, then there was no need to feel worried that they weren't doing anything. Hopefully

Auntie Mabel was right and her visions weren't going to come true.

She wondered what the others would say when she told them that Auntie Mabel knew all about magic.

"Good girl." Auntie Mabel's warm blue eyes met hers. "Remember, if you ever need advice about magic, you can always ask me."

Maia hugged her happily. "I will. Thank you so much, Auntie Mabel! Thank you!"

Chapter Five

Maia cycled quickly all the way home. As soon
as she got in, she ran to her bedroom, shut the
door and whispered Bracken's name.

Bracken appeared in the middle of her
rug and put his paws on her knees. "You're
excited," he said, his tail wagging.

"I *am*." Maia threw herself down on the
rug and told him all about Auntie Mabel.
"Oh, Bracken, she knew about the Star World.
Granny Anne *was* a Star Friend. She told
Auntie Mabel about it. Auntie Mabel said she

can do magic with crystals and stuff – she and Granny Anne used to work together."

Bracken flattened his ears, a troubled look on his face. "Oh."

"What's the matter?" Maia asked.

Bracken paced around. "Maia, people who aren't Star Friends aren't supposed to know about Star Animals. We were told when we came here that it was really important that the Star World was kept secret."

"But Auntie Mabel's really nice. She says she would have loved to be a Star Friend but she never got the chance," said Maia.

Bracken still looked anxious so Maia stroked him. "Please don't worry. Granny Anne wouldn't have told Auntie Mabel if she couldn't trust her. She gave me some tips on how to make my magic work better and she's going to see if she can find out if any dark magic is being used nearby." She tickled Bracken under the chin where his fur was really soft and fluffy. "Don't worry. Auntie Mabel is good – I know she is."

Bracken licked her cheek. "If you trust her then I do, too."

Maia remembered something else. "Auntie Mabel said the same as Sorrel – that the things I saw in the future might not be accurate because I'm only just beginning to learn how to use my magic," she said. "Maybe all those things I saw aren't going to happen and I just got it wrong." She looked at him hopefully.

Bracken rubbed his paw with his nose. "Maybe."

"And if it does turn out there is a Shade after all, we'll stop it," declared Maia.

"Definitely!" Bracken agreed.

Putting her arms round him, Maia felt a rush of happiness – when she was hugging Bracken everything was all right with the world.

✦ ✦ ✦

"Auntie Mabel knows about Star Animals and can do magic?" Sita echoed at break time the next day.

"Yes, she uses crystals to do magic!" Maia said. She, Ionie, Sita and Lottie were in a quiet spot at the far end of the playground, away from the school, where there was a grassy bank ending in a low wall. Two of the girls from Lottie's gymnastics team – Harriet and Elissa – were taking it in turns to walk along the wall as if it was a gymnastics beam. Maia and the others were standing a little way off, keeping their voices down.

Ionie had barely spoken to Maia, Lottie and Sita when they had got to school that morning. She was clearly still annoyed with them but the news about Auntie Mabel was far too interesting for her to resist. Now she joined the others as they crowded round

Maia, the argument forgotten.

"I can't believe this! What did she say about your visions?" Ionie demanded.

"That they're probably not going to come true," Maia whispered in relief. "She said she'll try to find out whether there is a Shade so we don't need to do anything for now. She'll use her crystals and—"

She was interrupted by a scream.

They swung round just in time to see Harriet crashing to the ground. She cried out in pain. For a fleeting second, Maia thought she saw something red and green racing through the bushes – but she didn't have time to look properly. Harriet needed help.

"My ankle!" Harriet gasped.

"I'll get a teacher!" said Elissa, sprinting off.

Sita crouched beside Harriet and touched her shoulder. "It's OK, you'll be all right," she said soothingly. "What happened? Did you lose your balance?"

"No. Someone pushed me!" Harriet said through her tears.

"Pushed you?" echoed Ionie.

"Yes," said Harriet. "I felt a shove."

"But there wasn't anyone near you," said Lottie.

"I felt it," Harriet insisted. Tears rolled down her cheeks. "What am I going to do? If my ankle's hurt I won't be able to do gymnastics."

Lottie, Ionie and Maia all glanced at Sita. Maia was sure the others were thinking the same as her. Could Sita heal Harriet? But Sita gave a small shake of her head, motioning with her eyes to the crowd of children beginning to gather. She couldn't risk healing Harriet in front of them.

Miss Harris came hurrying through the crowd. "Out of the way, everyone! Out of the way!"

She shooed Maia and the others back and crouched down beside Harriet, assessing her ankle. "Oh, Harriet. I think it might be broken," she said. "I'm going to call an ambulance." She pulled out her phone.

Maia felt a tap on her arm. It was Paige. The younger girl's eyes were wide. "What happened?" she whispered.

"She fell off the wall," Maia said. She remembered what Harriet had said about being pushed but there had been no one anywhere near. She must have imagined it … or maybe she made it up because she was embarrassed about falling. She was the best gymnast in the team.

"Is she going to be OK?" Paige asked.

"Miss Harris thinks her ankle might be broken," said Maia.

Miss Harris stood up. "Right, everyone. Go back to your classrooms, please."

As Maia followed the crowd back into school, she turned and looked over her shoulder. Harriet was on the ground still, hugging her injured ankle. Maia stopped dead, feeling shock run through her. It was the first image she'd seen in the mirror the day before!

"Maia?" Sita looked round at her. "Are you all right?"

Maia shook her head. "No," she whispered.

"What is it?" said Sita.

"When I was looking into the future yesterday, I saw someone on the ground holding their ankle – it was Harriet! I know it was!" The other images flashed through her mind – a girl falling from a climbing frame, Lottie looking terrified… Her blood turned to ice. "Oh, Sita – what if the things I saw *are* going to come true after all?"

CHAPTER SIX

School felt like it was never going to end. All day Maia kept thinking about the fact that the first vision she'd seen in the mirror had come true. News came back from the hospital after lunch that Harriet *had* broken her ankle. She wouldn't be able to do gymnastics for a couple of months.

The girls met in the playground after school.

"We have to talk," Maia told the others. "In private."

"Should we ask if we can go down to

the beach?" said Ionie. Now there were important things to discuss, she seemed to have completely got over her huff from the day before. "We could say we have to collect some shells for a project. There'll hardly be anyone there at this time of year."

"I'm supposed to be going to gymnastics," said Lottie. "But I could try telling my mum I'm too upset because of Harriet."

"Let's ask," said Maia.

They all ran off. Luckily their mums and dads agreed to them going to the beach provided they took their phones and were home before it got dark.

Leaving their bags and lunchboxes with their parents, they hurried through the village, crossed the road and headed down the lane. They passed Granny Anne's cottage and went on to where the lane ended in a small car park on the clifftop. It was a very blustery day with the sun only occasionally shining out from behind fast-moving pale-grey clouds. The cold salt-filled breeze whipped their hair around their faces and seagulls shrieked as they were tossed about by the wind.

"Come on," Maia said, heading down the stony track that led to the shingle beach. The tide was out and the beach was deserted apart from a couple of dog walkers in the distance.

"It's hard to hear!" Sita shouted above the wind as they stepped on to the shingle.

"Let's go to the base of the cliff," said Lottie. "It'll be more sheltered there."

They found a natural hollowed-out space with dry stones to sit on at the bottom of the cliff. They sat down, the cliff shielding them from the wind. "Do you think it's safe to call the Star Animals?" said Maia. She really wanted to talk to Bracken.

Ionie nodded. "No one usually comes this far down the beach. And if someone does come they can always vanish."

They all whispered their Star Animal's
name, and Bracken, Sorrel, Juniper and Willow
instantly appeared.

"Are you all right?" Bracken said, cuddling
into Maia's side. "You look worried."

"There was an accident at school," she told
him. They filled the animals in about what had
happened to Harriet.

"I wish I could have helped her," said Sita.
"But there were too many people around."

"Maybe you could help heal her now," said

Bracken eagerly.

Sorrel sighed. "The child has a broken ankle, fox. Doctors have seen her. Do you not think that the adult humans will ask questions if it miraculously heals?"

Bracken looked crestfallen. "Oh. I suppose so."

Maia put her arm round Bracken and pulled him close to her. "Listen, everyone. When I looked into the future yesterday, I saw Harriet after she'd hurt herself. I didn't know it was Harriet then because I couldn't see her face but now I know that the things I saw yesterday are coming true."

"Well, technically only *one* of them has come true," Sorrel said.

"If one has come true, the others might, too," said Maia. *Like the vision with Lottie in it*, she added in her head.

"Why don't you try again and find out what you see today?" said Bracken.

Maia pulled a small, round mirror out of her pocket. She'd found it in the drawer of her desk the night before – Granny Anne had given it to her a few years ago.

"Wait!" said Sorrel, leaping over to her. "I should check it to make sure there is no dark magic." She sniffed the mirror. "It's fine," she declared.

Maia took a breath and, cradling the mirror in her hands, she stared into it, opening herself to the magic current. She remembered Auntie Mabel's advice. If she wanted her magic to work well, she had to really concentrate.

Reveal the future to me, she commanded in her head.

A faint image appeared in the mirror. She stared hard at it but the more she tried to focus on it, the more indistinct it became.

Frustration welled inside her. "My magic's not working properly. I can't see the future."

Bracken licked her hand. "Why don't

you see if you can see what is happening somewhere else right now? That might be easier."

Maia sighed. "OK." She looked back into the mirror. *Show me something important that's happening right now,* she thought.

The surface of the mirror shivered and a picture appeared. It was Elissa playing on her climbing frame, climbing up to the top.

Fear gripped Maia. No! It was like the image she'd seen before. Only when she'd seen it yesterday it had been in the future and she hadn't been able to see who it was. Now it was happening for real. "Oh no," she breathed.

"What is it?" demanded Ionie.

Maia didn't answer. She was too busy watching Elissa, grabbing the top bar of the climbing frame with her hands and dangling happily. As she did so, there was a blur of colour above her and then suddenly Elissa cried out,

snatching one hand away from the bar as if
she'd been burned.

She dangled precariously from her other arm.

"Elissa!" gasped Maia as she watched her lose her grip and fall...

"What's happening, Maia?" demanded Lottie.

Maia saw Elissa tumble to the grass. She lay there for a few seconds before sitting up and starting to cry. She was cradling her wrist to her chest.

Maia looked up at the others. They were all staring at her.

"What is it?" said Sita. "What did you see?"

Maia gabbled out an explanation of what she had seen in the mirror. "It's Elissa. It looks like she's hurt her wrist," she finished.

Sorrel hissed. "Two girls hurt in one day. This is too much of a coincidence. I'm beginning to think you might be right, fox, and that there really must be a Shade involved."

Ionie got to her feet. "Sorrel, why don't you and I shadow-travel to Elissa's house and see if we can find any trace of one?"

"But what if someone sees you?" Sita said uneasily.

"We'll be careful. And we can't just sit around doing nothing." Ionie pushed her hands through her hair. "We're Star Friends, we're supposed to stop dark magic if it's happening!"

All Maia could think about was her third vision – the one where Lottie had been looking terrified. What if that came true, too? "I think Ionie's right – she and Sorrel should go."

Lottie looked anxious. "I think it's too dangerous. It would be better to go and talk to Auntie Mabel again and see if she's discovered anything."

"Maia could do that while Sorrel and I go shadow-travelling," said Ionie impatiently.

"Good idea," said Bracken.

"Not a good idea but an excellent one," said Sorrel, weaving through Ionie's legs.

The sun came out briefly, casting a patch of shadows at the foot of the rock. Ionie stepped into it. "Sorrel and I won't do anything apart from try and sense if a Shade is involved," she said. "I'll let you know what we find out tomorrow. Come on, Sorrel."

With that, they vanished.

Maia chewed her bottom lip. If her visions had been right then Lottie would be in danger next.

Bracken nuzzled her. "Don't worry, Maia," he said, seeming to read her thoughts. "We'll soon find out what's going on."

CHAPTER SEVEN

After saying goodbye to the animals, Maia, Lottie and Sita made their way back across the beach and up the lane. Lottie and Sita carried on home, while Maia went to Auntie Mabel's cottage. When she got there the lights were off but there was smoke coming from the chimney, which suggested someone was home. She knocked on the door but there was no answer.

Maia groaned inwardly and wished she could shadow-travel like Ionie – then she could go to wherever Auntie Mabel was.

Just as she reached her house, her phone pinged. Glancing at the screen, Maia saw a text from Ionie.

> Deffo a S at E's. We need to talk. Can u get to schl early 2moro? Ix

Maia's heart sank. For a moment she had a flashback to when they had been fighting the Mirror Shade and it had injured Bracken with its sharp knife-like fingers. Were they going to have to fight another Shade?

She typed a quick reply.

> See u 8.30 at schl. Tell the others. Mx

Slipping the phone into her pocket she opened the front door. As she stepped inside, she heard voices in the kitchen. Hope flared inside her. Was it Auntie Mabel?

But as she reached the kitchen door she saw that it was Paige and her mum. Paige was playing trains with Alfie on the floor, while her mum was having a cup of tea.

"Hi, sweetheart," Mrs Greene said to Maia.

"Did you get the shells you needed?"

"Shells?" Maia remembered they were supposed to have been collecting shells on the beach. "Oh yes, shells!" she said quickly. "Yep, we got everything we needed."

"These school projects," said Mrs Greene to Paige's mum. "There's always something else for them to do or find, isn't there?"

"Tell me about it," said Paige's mum with a groan.

"Mi-Mi!" Alfie said, holding up a train to Maia.

"Here's another tunnel, Alfie," said Paige, lifting her leg so Alfie could push a train underneath.

Just then, Paige's mum's phone buzzed. "Oh no," she said as she checked the message.

"What is it?" Mrs Greene asked in concern.

"You know Elissa who goes to gym with Paige? She's fallen off her climbing frame."

Paige swung round. "Is she hurt?"

"I'm afraid so." Her mum nodded as she reread the message. "Her mum says she's sprained her wrist. She's going to be off gym for at least a month."

"No!" Paige's hand flew to her mouth. "And Harriet hurt herself today, too." Her eyes filled with tears.

Poor Paige, Maia thought. Two of her friends getting hurt in one day. *We've got to stop this Shade.* She gave Paige a sympathetic look.

"I heard about Harriet," Mrs Greene said. "She broke her ankle, didn't she?"

Paige's mum nodded. "That's two members of the gymnastics team down. You're going to be in the display at this rate, Paige."

Paige gave a sob. "I don't want to be in it

just because people are getting hurt." She ran to her mum.

"Oh, Paigey." Her mum hugged her. "Don't cry. Your friends will be OK. They'll just be off gym for a while."

"It's a bit of a coincidence that they're both on the team, isn't it?" said Mrs Greene, shaking her head.

Maia felt like someone had just tipped a bucket of icy water over her head. Was it a coincidence that two girls on the team had both had accidents? Or was it *because* they were on the team?

"I'm just going upstairs," she said, heading to the door. She needed to talk to Bracken right away!

The moment she reached her bedroom, she shut the door and called Bracken's name. As soon as he appeared in front of her, she burst out, "Oh, Bracken. I've had such a horrible thought."

She sat down on the bed and told him. "What if someone's trying to hurt people on the team?" she finished.

"But who would do that?" said Bracken.

"I don't know," Maia said. "The team wins lots of competitions. Maybe … maybe someone in one of the other teams wants to try and stop them." She hugged him. "Bracken, if I'm right, Lottie could be in real danger. The Shade might be after her next."

Bracken nuzzled her cheek. "Don't worry. We'll find out what's going on and stop it."

Maia buried her face in his soft fur. "We have to!" she whispered.

The girls met in the playground before school. Maia was desperate to tell the others that she suspected the Shade was targeting the gym team but she didn't want to upset Lottie. And what if she was wrong?

Luckily Ionie took charge. Looking like she could hardly contain her excitement, she dragged them over to the wall.

"OK, so last night this is what happened," she whispered to them. "Sorrel and I shadow-travelled to Elissa's garden and Sorrel smelled that a Shade had been on the climbing frame. For definite. Sorrel said it was a really strong smell. So then we decided to come here – to school – and Sorrel smelled the same scent here, too. Somehow *the same Shade* caused both Harriet and Elissa's accidents!"

"What do we do?" Sita said.

"We need to find out what type of Shade it is," said Ionie.

"And how it caused the accidents," said Lottie.

"And what object it's trapped in," added Ionie. She glanced at Maia. "You're being quiet today."

"I'm just thinking about it all," Maia said. She glanced around at the busy playground. She wanted to wait until Bracken and the other animals were there before they worked out how to find out more about the Shade. "I think we should go to the clearing after school."

Lottie nodded. "I was wondering if you could use your magic to try and look back at the accidents – you might be able to see how the Shade caused them."

"Brilliant idea!" said Ionie.

Lottie looked surprised at the praise.

"All of you ask if you can come to my house

after school," Ionie went on. "We'll go to the clearing and Maia can use her magic."

Sita nodded. "Then maybe we'll find out what's going on."

To Maia's relief, nothing happened to Lottie that day at school. She decided she would tell the others about the third vision when they got to the clearing and could talk about it properly, with the Star Animals there, too. She watched the clock, willing the school day to be over.

"What? You four want to meet up *again*?" Maia's mum said when Maia ran over to her in the playground and asked if she could go to Ionie's house. "Don't you see enough of each other in school? Well, OK, I guess. Be back by teatime though." Maia nodded. "Now, did you ask everyone if they want to sleep over tomorrow night? Should I go and have a quick word with their parents?"

"Oh." With everything that had happened, Maia had completely forgotten about the sleepover. "I … um … asked Lottie and Sita," she said. "They can come."

"And Ionie?" Mrs Greene said.

"I haven't asked her yet," Maia admitted.

"Her dad's over there. I'll go and ask him." Mrs Greene headed off and Maia went to join Ionie and Sita.

"Mum said it's fine for me to go to your house," said Maia. "Also, I'm going to have a sleepover at mine tomorrow," she said to Ionie. "Do you want to come?"

Ionie's face lit up. "A sleepover? Yes, please!"

Maia felt guilty about not mentioning it sooner. Ionie hadn't been anything like as annoying the last few days. She'd even been nicer in class. Maybe Sita had been right about her just really wanting to be friends.

Lottie came running over. "Mum says I can be out for an hour but then she's going to pick me up because I've got a piano lesson and she won't let me miss it. Come on. Let's go."

They dumped their bags at Ionie's house, grabbed a packet of crisps and an apple each, and then set off down the lane towards the clearing.

"OK, I've been thinking about the accidents and what we can do…" Ionie began.

"Shh," said Maia, spotting a woman riding up the hill towards them on a big grey horse.

Ionie lowered her voice so the rider couldn't hear. "The most important thing is to find out what object the Shade is trapped inside. Then we can try and get hold of it and—"

Before she could finish her sentence, they heard the horse rider shout out. Looking up, they saw the horse rearing up on its back legs. The rider grabbed for the reins but as she struggled to keep control of the horse, she lost her balance and fell to the ground. The horse bolted towards the girls at a gallop.

"Watch out!" yelled Ionie. She grabbed Sita and Maia, who were on either side of her, and pulled them to the side of the lane.

To Maia it seemed as if time slowed down. The horse's hooves clattered on the stones,

its nostrils flaring as it thundered up the lane. Maia thought she caught sight of a flash of red and green in the bushes at the side of the lane, but she only registered it for a second before she realized the horse was galloping straight at Lottie.

"Lottie!" gasped Maia as she saw her friend's eyes widen in fear.

Chapter Eight

Maia felt magic rush through her. She saw the horse's glowing outline starting to swerve to the right to avoid Lottie but at that exact moment Lottie made to dive the same way to try and get out of its path.

"Go the other way, Lottie!" shrieked Maia.

Lottie's magic must have been coursing through her, too. In the blink of an eye she had thrown herself to the other side, somersaulted in the air and jumped to her feet, unhurt.

The horse swerved just as Maia had seen it

would. It stumbled and regained its balance then slowed and came to a stop. It stood trembling at the side of the lane, its sides heaving. Sita ran over to it and took its reins. She touched the horse's neck and murmured to it. Maia saw the horse's breathing steady and its eyes start to lose their panicked look as Sita's magic began to calm it.

The rider came running up the lane. "Oh my goodness. Are you all OK?"

"Yes, we're fine," said Lottie, although she looked very shaken.

"I don't know what just happened. Duke's never reared or galloped off like that. Something in the bushes must have spooked him."

Maia remembered the flash of movement she had seen and peered into the undergrowth. With the magic running through her, she could see every leaf, every twig and every branch, but there was nothing unusual. Still, *something* had made the horse rear. Something red and green…

Sita led the horse over. He nuzzled his rider on the arm.

"You silly thing, what was all that about?" his rider said. She gave the girls a relieved look. "I'm glad you're safe. I thought he was going to knock you down," she said to Lottie. "I'm really sorry if he scared you."

"Don't worry," said Lottie. "I'm all right."

Luckily, Maia thought in her head.

The rider said goodbye, mounted and rode off.

Maia glanced round at the others. "We need to talk."

★ ★ ★

As soon as they ran into the clearing, the animals appeared.

"What's happened?" Bracken said, looking at Maia's face.

Maia hugged him and drew in a deep breath. She felt better now that he was with her. Looking up, she saw that the others were close to their animals, too – Juniper was on Lottie's shoulder, Sita was hugging Willow and even Sorrel, who was normally so haughty, had jumped on to Ionie's lap.

Maia began to tell Bracken about the incident with the horse and the others chipped in, too.

"If Maia hadn't yelled at me to jump the other way then that horse would have knocked me down," said Lottie.

Juniper jumped round to her other shoulder in concern. "Do you think someone was trying to hurt you?"

Lottie swallowed. "I suppose it *could* just have been an accident."

Sorrel jumped off Ionie's lap. "If a Shade caused that horse to bolt, I'll be able to smell it on the lane." She leaped into the bushes.

They waited anxiously until Sorrel came bounding back out of the bushes, her tail puffed up. "A Shade *was* there," she said with a hiss. "The same one. That horse galloping at Lottie was no accident."

"We need to do something!" said Ionie.

"I don't want to fight a Shade again," Sita said in a shaky voice.

Willow nuzzled her comfortingly.

"Um… I think I need to tell you something," Maia said. "The three visions I saw in the mirror have all come true and we now know the accidents all involve the same Shade. Well, I think they're linked and that someone is deliberately trying to hurt people on the gym team."

They all stared at her.

"On the gym team?" echoed Lottie.

"Of course," breathed Ionie. "Harriet, Elissa and Lottie are all on the gym team."

"But why would someone want to hurt people on the team?" Lottie said.

"Could it be someone in a rival team?" Bracken said.

"No! The teams are competitive but none of them would want to hurt someone else," said Lottie.

"But someone's responsible for this," said Juniper.

"We have to find out who it is," said Sita.

Ionie caught her breath. "Maia – why don't you ask the magic to show you!"

"I can try," said Maia eagerly.

She pulled the mirror out of her pocket and opened her mind to the magic. As it tingled through her, she concentrated hard, like Auntie Mabel had told her, and thought, *Show me the person conjuring the Shade that hurt Harriet and Elissa and tried to hurt Lottie.*

The mirror flickered and then went dark.

Maia blinked. "That's weird."

"What's going on?" asked Sita. "What can you see?"

"Nothing. The mirror's just gone black. What does it mean, Bracken?"

The fox looked worried. "The person using dark magic may have cast a spell so they can't be seen by magic."

"Oh." Maia's hopes deflated. "Well, how about I try and see the Shade?" she said. "If I ask to see it, maybe we'll find out what object it's trapped in."

"Good idea!" said Ionie.

Maia took a breath and focused on the mirror again. *Show me the Shade who made the horse bolt*, she thought.

The darkness faded and a picture appeared in the mirror. There was an expanse of green lawn, some trees, a bench and a shed in the distance.

"What can you see?" asked Lottie eagerly.

"A garden," said Maia in surprise.

"Is there anything there that might have a Shade trapped inside it?" asked Bracken.

"No, there's just grass and trees and plants," Maia said.

"There must be something there," said Sorrel impatiently. "Look harder."

"I am looking," said Maia in frustration. "I can't see anything."

"Could the Shade be invisible?" suggested Sita.

"No," said Bracken. "Some Shades can move very fast but they're not invisible."

Ionie sighed. "This isn't getting us anywhere."

"It's not Maia's fault!" Lottie said defensively.

"Ionie didn't say it was," Sita said quickly. "Why don't you try looking at the accidents? Maybe we can work out how the Shade caused them," she said to Maia.

Maia hesitated. She hadn't yet managed to look into the past. Could she do it now? She remembered Auntie Mabel's advice about needing to really focus. Staring at the mirror and frowning in concentration she whispered, "Show me Harriet's accident."

A blurry image started to appear in the mirror. Maia peered closer. *Work*, she thought. *Work now.* But the picture only grew more blurry.

"I can't do it!" she told the others. She willed the mirror to show more but the image remained fuzzy.

Bracken nuzzled her. "Don't worry. Looking into the past is hard."

To Maia's surprise, Sorrel nodded. "The fox is right. Don't feel frustrated, child."

"We'll have to think of some other way to find out what's going on," said Lottie. She glanced at her watch. "I'm going to have to go. Mum's meeting me at Ionie's soon. I can't be late."

"But what about the Shade?" said Ionie.

"It'll have to wait until tomorrow," said Lottie. "We'll have lots of time to try and find out what's going on when we're at Maia's for the sleepover."

"Good idea," said Sita. "Come on. Let's all walk back together. You shouldn't be on your own, Lottie, in case something else happens."

Maia swallowed down her frustration. She didn't want to have to wait until the next day. She wanted to do something right then and there. She'd just have to try even harder, as Auntie Mabel had said. Thinking that made her realize that she still hadn't asked Auntie Mabel if she had discovered anything. *I'll go and see her on the way home*, Maia decided.

✦ ✦ ✦

On the way to Auntie Mabel's, Maia texted her mum.

> Finished at Ionie's. Going 2 c Auntie Mabel. Is that OK? Mxx

A text quickly pinged back.

> That's nice of you. I think she's lonely without Granny Anne. I'll pick you up from there. xxx

Maia hurried up the road. This time the

lights were on at Auntie Mabel's house and she was dusting a display of glittering crystals and stones that were on the windowsill in the lounge. Spotting Maia through the window, Auntie Mabel waved and came to open the front door.

"Maia! Come in."

Maia followed her inside.

"So, what's been going on? Let me get some drinks and biscuits, and you can tell me everything," Auntie Mabel said. She bustled around, fetching a tray and glasses.

Soon they were sitting in the lounge beside the log burner. Maia started to tell Auntie Mabel everything that had been happening.

"That's awful!" said Auntie Mabel, looking shocked when Maia told her about the horse bolting up the lane. "Poor Lottie must have been so scared."

"She was. It was a Shade that caused it. Sorrel went back and she sensed one had been there."

Maia nibbled a biscuit. "Have you managed to find out anything, Auntie Mabel?"

Auntie Mabel sighed. "I'm afraid not. The crystals aren't showing me anything. I just see darkness when I try and look."

Maia felt a rush of disappointment. "That's what happened when I tried to look. Bracken says the person who trapped the Shade must have cast a spell to stop themselves being seen."

"Yes, that's what I've been thinking, too," said Auntie Mabel quickly. "Well, I guess all we can do is keep on trying. This can't be allowed to continue."

"Thank you," said Maia. Just knowing Auntie Mabel was trying to help made her feel better.

"Tell me as soon as you discover anything else," said Auntie Mabel.

"I will," Maia said.

There was a knock on the door. "That's probably my mum," said Maia.

"No more talking about magic then," said Auntie Mabel with a smile. "And I'd better make a fresh pot of tea."

Chapter Nine

When Maia got up the next morning, she tried using her magic to see the local gym clubs in her bedroom mirror, to check whether there was anything suspicious going on. But all she saw were teams practising their routines.

Halfway through the morning, her mum knocked on her door and looked into her room.

Maia hurriedly picked up her phone as if she were writing a message.

"Come on," her mum said. "You've

been shut in here too long. Time to come downstairs. You can help me tidy up."

"OK," said Maia reluctantly.

Her mum shook her head. "You girls and your phones. You're on them far too much."

Maia thought what her mum would say if she told her she hadn't been on her phone, she'd been using magic!

She helped tidy up and then got ready for the sleepover. By three o'clock everything was sorted. Her bedroom floor was covered with squishy duvets and pillows. She had been to the newsagents and bought sweets for a midnight feast, and her mum had helped her make some cinder toffee. It was cooling downstairs in the kitchen beside a bag of giant fluffy white marshmallows for toasting on the bonfire her dad had built in the back garden.

"Make sure you save some marshmallows for me," said Clio as she came into the kitchen and helped herself to a piece of cinder toffee.

"What time are you babysitting Paige today?" Maia asked.

"I'm going over there now and staying until eight o'clock," said Clio. "I wish I wasn't. There's a music awards ceremony on TV that I really want to watch. Maybe Paige will watch it with me. Or why don't you come round? You could play with her while I watch it."

"I can't. Lottie, Sita and Ionie will be here any minute," said Maia.

Clio sighed and grabbed her bag from the

side. "All right. See you later."

"Bye!" Maia called, as Clio opened the front door.

"Oh, hi there, Ionie," Maia heard Clio say. "Maia's in the kitchen. Go on through."

Maia went into the hall as Ionie came in. She had a spotty blue bag with her. "Hi," Maia said. "Shall we take your bag up to my room?"

Ionie nodded. As they went upstairs she whispered to Maia, "Was Auntie Mabel able to tell you anything new?"

Maia shook her head. They went into the room and shut the door behind them. "Auntie Mabel hasn't been able to find out anything."

Ionie dropped her bag on one of the duvets. "I couldn't sleep last night. I kept thinking about it all. Sorrel and I shadow-travelled a bit, and tried to see if we could find any other traces of dark magic."

"Did you find anything?" Maia asked eagerly.

"Not much. Sorrel got a strong scent of it up near the main road but she thinks that might have been from when the Shade tried to hurt Lottie. The scent faded when we travelled further into the village. Have you tried using your magic again?" Ionie asked.

"Yes, but looking at people in rival gym teams hasn't shown me anything useful, and when I try and look back at the accidents to see if I can find any clues, it's really blurry. I wish I could do it. I'm trying to concentrate really hard, just like Auntie Mabel told me to, but it's not working."

Ionie frowned. "Auntie Mabel told you to do that? I find my magic works best when I just relax."

"Auntie Mabel said you need to relax when you first connect with your magic but afterwards it's better if you try to really focus."

"Weird. Maybe her type of magic is different…" Ionie said, puzzled.

"I guess so," said Maia.

"Why don't you try what I do? I slowly count down from ten to zero and focus on my breathing, letting everything fade away, then I get this feeling of my magic getting stronger and stronger – it feels like a current of power surging through me," said Ionie. "It might work for you, too."

Just then the doorbell rang. "I bet that'll be Lottie and Sita," Maia said.

After Mrs Greene and Sita's mum had chatted for a few minutes and said their goodbyes, the four girls ran upstairs. Maia shut the door and all the animals appeared.

"Together at last!" said Bracken, jumping round happily as Juniper scampered along Maia's curtain pole and Willow butted her head affectionately against Sita's legs.

Sorrel stalked into the centre of the room. "When you've all finished behaving like three-week-old kittens, can we get started?"

"I hope everyone else on the gym team is OK," said Sita. "Have you heard about anyone else being injured, Lottie?"

"No. The whole team was at training this morning," said Lottie. "And the two replacements. Paige was there with them – she's the top of the reserve list now, so if anyone else gets injured, she'll be on the team."

"I bet she's pleased," said Maia.

Lottie frowned. "It was strange. She was really quiet today."

"I hope she's all right," said Sita.

"Why don't you use magic to check on her, Maia?" suggested Bracken.

Maia nodded and took her mirror out of her pocket. "Paige," she whispered.

The surface of the mirror flickered and an image of Paige appeared. It was slightly fuzzy. Remembering what Ionie had said, Maia took a breath and counted back from ten, letting the magic flow through her without trying to force it. To her delight the image grew sharper and sharper.

Paige was sitting on a garden bench. Her knees were pulled up to her chin and there were tears rolling down her cheeks. She looked like she was whispering to herself.

"I can see her," Maia told the others. "She's in her garden. She looks really upset."

"Can you see anything else?" Bracken urged.

Maia studied the image intently. She let everything else around her fade away and gradually made out the words that Paige was whispering to herself. "I want it to stop. I'm scared."

Maia's skin prickled. She was about to tell the others when her eyes caught a movement behind Paige. The leaves of the plants quivered as if something was edging towards the bench.

"There's something in the garden with Paige!" Maia said anxiously. "It's creeping towards her."

"What is it?" demanded Ionie.

"I can't see," said Maia. "It's hidden by the shrubs."

"What if it's the Shade?" said Sita.

"We have to go to her!" said Bracken.

"I'll shadow-travel there," said Ionie.

"No, we should stay together!" Lottie said.

But Ionie was already at the edge of the

room where there was a faint shadow cast by the afternoon sun. "Come on, Sorrel!" she cried. The second she stepped into the shadows, she disappeared and then Sorrel vanished, too.

"I can't believe she just did that!" burst out Lottie.

Maia could. If she'd been Ionie, she'd have done the same. "We can't let her go there alone. We have to go, too," she said.

"None of us can shadow-travel," said Sita.

"Maybe not," said Maia, pulling her bedroom door open. "But we can run!"

Chapter Ten

By the time Maia, Lottie and Sita reached Paige's house, they were all gasping for breath. Maia's heart thundered in her chest. What were they going to find? What if something had happened to Paige – or Ionie? She wished she could call Bracken to her side but she couldn't risk anyone seeing him.

The three of them raced round the side of the house and into the back garden. To the right there was a small orchard of eight apple trees. In the centre of the lawn there was a stone birdbath on a plinth and a wooden garden shed with an open door at the end of the garden. On the far side of the garden was the bench Maia had seen Paige sitting on. But there was no sign of the younger girl now.

"There's Ionie!" said Lottie, pointing into the orchard.

Ionie was standing in the shadows of the trees with a garden rake in her hands, looking warily at the bushes.

Maia felt a rush of relief. Ionie was OK. She ran through the trees towards Ionie with Lottie and Sita following her. "Ionie! What's going on?" she hissed as Ionie swung round to look at her.

"Why did you just go off like that?" said Lottie.

"Because it sounded like Paige was in danger," said Ionie.

"Where is Paige?" asked Sita anxiously.

"Inside. Just as I arrived, Clio came to the French windows and called her in." Ionie continued to scan the garden. "There's something moving in the bushes. It's small and I caught a glimpse of red and green. I grabbed this rake from the shed in case it attacked me."

"It must be the Shade!" said Maia. "I saw a red and green blur at each of the accidents."

A scuttling sound in the branches above them suddenly interrupted her. They all looked up. "What's that?" said Lottie.

Sita screamed as the branches parted and a pottery face grinned down at them. Its eyes glowed red beneath its bobble hat.

"It's the garden gnome!" cried Lottie.

"A wish was made. It has to come true!" the gnome hissed. "I will hurt one of you!"

"Oh no, you won't!" said Ionie fiercely, lashing out with the rake, trying to hit him.

The gnome cackled and jumped hard on the branch he was standing on.

CRACK! The branch broke and fell, crashing down right on to Lottie and hitting her head. Crying out, she crumpled to the ground.

"Lottie!" Sita gasped.

The gnome jumped down and ran off. Maia and Ionie crouched beside Sita. There was a deep gash on Lottie's forehead but she was trying to sit up.

"Let me help," Sita said. "I can heal you." She gently touched Lottie's head near the cut and the wound began to close. The pain faded from Lottie's face but she still looked dazed.

"My head," she said, reaching to touch the place where the wound had been.

"I've healed it," said Sita.

"That was amazing, Sita," Ionie said.

"Are you all right, Lottie?" Maia asked quickly.

"I think so, I just feel dizzy," said Lottie, blinking. "What happened?"

"The gnome made the branch break," said Maia. "It hit your head."

"So the Shade is in the gnome," said Ionie. "It must have been going about hurting people on the gym team. But why?"

"I've no idea. But what's more important is stopping it before it hurts someone else." Lottie tried to stand but her legs buckled.

"You need to rest," Sita said, catching her.

"Why don't you both stay here while Maia and I try to find it?" said Ionie. "You could wait in the shed. There are a couple of chairs in there and lots of garden tools you could use to defend yourselves if the gnome comes."

"I want to come with you," said Lottie, but she swayed as she stood up again.

"Lottie, you can't," said Maia.

"Come to the shed with me, Lottie," said Sita. She looked into Lottie's eyes. "Come on," she said softly.

The stubbornness slowly faded from Lottie's face. "OK," she said obediently.

Maia gave Sita a quick smile – her magic was getting stronger all the time.

Leaving Sita to help Lottie into the shed, Maia and Ionie ran across the lawn to the house. "What if it's gone after Paige?" whispered Maia.

There were big French windows that led

from the garden into the house. Maia peered through them and breathed a sigh of relief. Paige was sitting on one of the sofas with Clio. There was no sign of the creepy gnome.

Maia knocked lightly on the window. Paige jumped. Clio smiled and beckoned them in. "Hi, have you come round to see Paige?" she said as they opened the doors.

"Um … yeah," said Maia.

"Good. I think she needs a distraction. Don't you, Paige?"

Paige didn't say anything.

"Are you OK?" Maia said to her, but Paige still didn't speak.

"She's a bit upset," Clio explained. "She was just telling me that a horse nearly knocked Lottie over yesterday."

Maia frowned. How did Paige know about that?

"Don't worry, Paige," said Ionie. "Lottie's fine."

"But something else might happen to her,"

Paige said fearfully.

"I'm sure it won't," Clio reassured her.

"But it might!" Paige burst out. "And if it does, it'll all be my fault!" She jumped up and ran out of the room and up the stairs.

Clio stood up. "I don't know what's the matter with her today," she said. "I've never known her like this."

Paige's words echoed uneasily in Maia's head. What did she mean? Why did she think it would be her fault?

"Would you like us to talk to her?" Ionie offered.

"I should probably do it," said Clio, glancing longingly at the TV.

"Don't worry. We'll go," said Maia.

"OK then," said Clio, settling back down. "If you need me, give me a shout. Where are Lottie and Sita?" she said, looking around.

"Outside in the garden," said Maia truthfully. "We'll go and see if Paige is OK."

Exchanging looks, she and Ionie hurried out of the room. They heard Clio turn up the sound on the TV as they ran up the wide sweeping staircase. The house was very big, with two floors of bedrooms and bathrooms above the ground floor. The lights were off on the stairs and landing, and it was quite dark and gloomy. Maia's skin prickled. Light was shining out from underneath Paige's bedroom door. They hurried towards it.

Maia knocked. "Can we come in, Paige?"

"OK." Paige's voice was tearful.

They pushed open the door and went in. The walls were covered with pictures of gymnasts. Paige was sitting on her bed, hugging an old teddy bear.

Maia wished Sita was there – she always knew what to say when people were upset. She glanced at Ionie, who cleared her throat.

"Um … what's the matter, Paige?" Ionie said.

"I can't tell you," said Paige. She pulled her knees up to her chest and buried her head in them.

Maia went over rather awkwardly and sat down beside her. "What did you mean when you said Lottie would get hurt and it would all be your fault?"

"I meant what I said. It's my fault that Harriet and Elissa are hurt, and if Lottie gets hurt that will be my fault as well…" Paige broke off with a sob.

"It isn't your fault. It really isn't," said Maia, patting Paige's shoulder. She looked at Ionie but Ionie just shrugged. She was no better than Maia at comforting people.

"It is my fault!" Paige burst out. "He told me I was really good at gymnastics and that I should be on the team. He told me he could make my wish come true and I should wish I was on the gym team. I thought it would bring me good luck – I didn't think he'd bring everyone else *bad* luck!"

"Who are you talking about?" Ionie asked.

"The garden gnome!"

Maia's eyes met Ionie's in shock.

"He can talk," Paige went on with another sob. "I know you won't believe me but he's a gnome who can grant wishes, and ever since I wished to be on the team, he's been hurting people. He told me today that he'd made a horse gallop at Lottie but it hadn't worked so he was going to try and do something else."

"Oh, Paige," said Maia, her heart thudding.

"I said I wished I'd never made the wish," said Paige. "I said I didn't wish it any more but he just laughed and told me that once a wish has been made it can't be stopped." She looked up. "Do you believe me?"

"Yes, we do – and we're going to help sort it out," said Ionie. "Where's the gnome now, Paige?"

"I … I don't know." Paige gulped. "He moves really fast. One minute he's there, the next he isn't."

"We'll find him," said Maia. She gave Paige a hug. "Run downstairs, shut the door, close the curtains and stay in the lounge until we come and find you. Don't say a word to Clio. Promise?"

Paige nodded. "Promise," she said, her eyes wide.

They ran along the landing with her. Reaching the staircase, they watched her go into the warm, bright lounge and shut the door behind her.

Maia took a deep breath. "Are you ready for some gnome-hunting?" she asked.

Ionie's eyes gleamed as they met hers. "Bring it on!"

CHAPTER ELEVEN

"So, where do we start looking?" whispered Ionie, glancing around the first-floor landing.

"I'm not sure," said Maia.

They moved slowly along the corridor.

Something red and green raced out of a nearby bedroom. It passed them in a blur and scuttled up the staircase that led to the top floor.

"There it is!" gasped Maia.

Ionie was already running up the stairs, taking them two at a time. Maia charged after her.

They reached the top and stopped. There was a long landing with rooms leading off it but no sign of the gnome.

"Bracken!" whispered Maia. "I need you." There was a shimmer in the air and suddenly Bracken was there beside her. Ionie whispered Sorrel's name and the next moment, the wildcat appeared, too.

"Ionie, what's going on?" demanded Sorrel. "I can smell the Shade everywhere."

The girls explained in hurried whispers, their eyes darting around the landing as they spoke.

"The gnome must have a Wish Shade in it," said Bracken, the hackles on his neck rising. "Wish Shades work on people's worst feelings, getting them to make wishes and then bringing them true in horrible ways."

"Paige is really upset," said Maia. "She didn't mean for all the accidents to happen."

"And now the Shade won't stop until her

wish has been granted," said Sorrel. "We have to find that gnome."

"It came up the stairs. It must be here somewhere," said Maia.

"We'll catch it," Bracken growled. "It's not going to get away."

"For once you and I are in complete agreement, fox," said Sorrel. Her tail fluffed out like a brush and she prowled forwards. Ionie moved silently beside her, and Maia and Bracken followed.

Opening her mind, Maia let magic flow into her. Every cell in her body felt as if it was on red alert. Where was the gnome hiding?

A sinister giggle echoed out of a room halfway down the corridor.

Sorrel and Bracken bounded forwards, moving as one. They leaped into the room with Ionie and Maia hot on their heels.

They were in a spare bedroom with a double bed, wardrobe and a large window that looked on to the garden. Maia glanced around the room. Her eyes met Ionie's. They nodded at each other in silent agreement and edged further into the room, matching each other step for step. Maia opened the wardrobe while Ionie checked inside the drawers.

"Where are you, Shade?" growled Bracken.

The gnome burst out from behind the curtains with a cackle. "Made you look! Made you stare!" he crowed, his eyes glowing red. "Now it's time to give *someone* a scare!" Throwing himself at the bed, he bounced on it and somersaulted over their heads. Sorrel flung herself upwards but her claws

just missed the gnome's head. He landed and
rolled on the floor. Bracken leaped at him
but the gnome was too fast. He darted out of
the room. Bracken barked in frustration and
chased after the gnome, with Ionie, Sorrel and
Maia close behind. He ran into a room at the
end of the corridor, slamming the door shut
behind him.

Ionie slowly turned the handle and pushed open the door, revealing a room with a desk and filing cabinets. But the gnome was nowhere to be seen.

Bracken put his nose to the floor as if following a scent and padded over to the open window. He put his paws on the window ledge and looked out. "I think he's gone out through the window."

Sorrel followed him and sniffed the air. "You're right. He's not here any more."

"I thought he said he was going to scare us – not run away," said Ionie, puzzled. She turned to Maia. "Can you use your magic to find out where he's gone?"

Maia pulled the mirror out of her pocket and kneeled down on the floor.

"I want to see where the gnome is now," she whispered.

An image appeared in the mirror. It looked like the back of a wooden shed. The gnome was heading towards it, a burning branch in his hand. More branches had been piled behind the shed like a bonfire.

"The gnome's trying to set light to the shed!" she exclaimed. "He must still be trying to make Paige's wish come true by hurting Lottie. He led us up here because he wanted us out of the way."

"Of course!" gasped Ionie. "It's Lottie he's after, not us! We have to stop him!"

They all raced out of the room and down the stairs and out through the kitchen door.

The sun was low in the sky now. The smell of woodsmoke drifted towards them from the fire behind the shed and Maia could hear the faint crackle of burning branches. Once the fire took hold it would spread to the wooden sides of the shed.

Ionie charged towards the shed. "Sita! Lottie! Get out of there!"

Bracken and Sorrel raced ahead of her.

Bracken leaped for the door handle and tried to turn it with his teeth but the door wouldn't open.

"It's bolted!" he barked.

Maia ran up to the door while Ionie ran to a big water butt at the side and started to fill a bucket with water to try and douse the bonfire. Hearing the commotion, Lottie and Sita appeared at the small window.

"I can smell smoke," Sita said. "What's happening?"

"You've got to get out!" Maia shouted frantically. "The shed's going to catch fire any minute!" She started tugging at the bolt that had been pushed across the door on the outside. The bolt was stiff but she managed to pull it back and yanked the door open.

For a second Maia saw the relief on Sita and Lottie's faces, and then Sita's eyes widened in horror as she looked at something behind Maia.

"The gnome!" she cried.

Maia heard a cackle and felt herself being shoved in the back. Losing her balance, she fell inside the shed. Before she knew what was happening, the door had been slammed shut and she heard the bolt being pushed back across on the outside.

"Now I've got you! Now you're caught! Now a lesson you'll be taught!" she heard the gnome crowing.

"What's going on?" Lottie demanded, helping Maia to her feet.

Maia registered with relief that Lottie looked completely back to normal. Juniper was jumping round the walls and Willow was trembling by the door.

"The gnome's trying to burn down the shed," said Maia desperately. "We have to get out of here!" She hammered on the door. "Ionie! Unbolt the door!" Her heart pounded as the first tendrils of smoke started to fill the shed.

"Look!" said Lottie, pointing out of the window. The gnome was in front of the door.

Ionie was facing him, hands on hips, the bucket at her feet. "Let my friends out!" she demanded.

"No!" the gnome sniggered.

Ionie's eyes narrowed. "I command…"

In a flash the gnome turned his back on her. "I can't see you!"

"She has to be looking into his eyes to be able to command him," said Bracken, his paws on the window ledge.

The gnome said, "I know you want to send me back to the shadows. But I'm having far too much fun in the human world to go back there." He paused. "Now, let's think about you, Ionie. When this shed burns down I'll have granted Paige's wish to be on the gym team. Maybe *you* would like some help next." His voice became soft and persuasive. "What could I help you with? Maia, maybe... You *really* wish you could be her, don't you?"

Maia frowned. What was he talking about?

"I don't know what you mean," said Ionie, shooting a nervous glance at the shed.

"I can see your thoughts." The gnome moved backwards, getting closer to her but being careful not to make eye contact. "Everyone likes Maia, don't they? She's Little Miss Popular. She doesn't even seem to try and *still* people like her. It's not fair, is it? You could be like that, though. One wish and she will get all the bad luck." He gave a sly giggle.

"Now what do you say?" He rubbed his hands together greedily.

"Well … I suppose you do have a point," said Ionie.

"No," Maia whispered.

"I mean, it is really tempting," Ionie said, wandering back towards the orchard.

The gnome cackled and edged closer still, moving away from the shed door. "I know. All you have to do is make one little wish."

"One wish," echoed Ionie. She reached the shadows of the trees and spun round. "I know what I'd like to wish for." She vanished.

The gnome spluttered in shock.

In the blink of an eye, Ionie appeared in the shadows of the shed by the door. "I wish for my friends to be free! And, hey, I don't even need your magic to do it!" She pulled back the bolt and opened the door.

Maia, Lottie and Sita charged out of the shed, the Star Animals at their sides. As they ran, they all drew on their Star Magic. Instantly Maia could see everything in incredible detail.

"No!" shrieked the gnome, leaping on to the birdbath in the centre of the lawn. "I will hurt you!" he screamed, pointing at Lottie. "I will grant Paige's wish!"

"I don't think so!" Juniper said, jumping off Lottie's shoulder and grabbing a fallen apple in his mouth. He scampered up her leg and nudged it into her hand. "Time to hit a real target, Lottie! Knock him off the birdbath!"

Lottie drew back her arm then chucked the apple at the gnome. It shot through the air with perfect accuracy and hit him square on the forehead. "Bullseye!" she whooped as the gnome lost his balance and fell backwards.

There was a cracking noise as he broke into pieces.

A cloud of darkness rose from the shattered pieces of pottery and formed into a tall figure. His nose and chin were pointed and his eyes glowed red. Threadbare clothes hung off his angular body.

"I am free!" he hissed in delight, his voice shivering through the air. As he spoke, his body became more and more solid. "I can go where I want and do as I will. I shall do whatever I like."

Bracken raced towards him. "No, you won't! I'll stop you!"

Maia's heart leaped into her mouth. "Bracken! Come back!"

"Say the words, Ionie," said Sorrel, her back arching.

Ionie pointed her finger at the Shade. "I command you to…"

"No! I will not be commanded! I will not be sent back!" The Shade started to stride away but Bracken reached him. With a growl, he bit the Shade's leg and hung on tight. The Shade hissed and swiped down with his sharp claws. With the magic coursing through her, Maia saw where the Shade's hand was going to land an instant before it did. "Bracken! Go left!" she yelled.

Bracken flung himself to the left just in time. The Shade

missed him. Bracken tumbled over on to his back. Maia watched as the Shade lifted its arm to strike the fox. She raced forwards. "No! You won't hurt Bracken!"

But Sorrel, Willow and Juniper were even faster. With two bounds Sorrel sprang up on to the Shade's back. "Stop right there, Shade!" she hissed, her claws digging in. The Shade howled and swung this way and that, trying to shake her off.

Juniper dashed in front of the Shade's feet, tripping him over. He stumbled to his knees. Willow butted the Shade in the chest with her head, sending him sprawling on to its back.

Lottie was beside him in the blink of an eye. As the Shade started to sit up, she jumped on to his chest, pushing his shoulders back down again. He hissed in fury and arched his back.

"A bit of help here!" Lottie gasped.

Maia reached the Shade at the same moment Sita did. Flinging themselves down they each grabbed one of the Shade's bony arms, pinning his hands down.

"No!" he shrieked, thrashing from side to side.

Maia could feel her grip loosening. She couldn't hold on much longer. And then suddenly Ionie was there, leaning over the Shade and looking into his red eyes.

"I command you to return to the Shadows!" she said before he could close his eyes.

With a strangled cry the Shade started to dissolve into shadow. He twisted and turned as he became smaller and smaller. "This is not the end," he hissed. "She will find ways to bring misery. She will call more of us forth from the Shadows even though one of you has more power than she can dream of!" With a final hiss he faded away to nothing.

There was a moment's silence. "What was all that about?" Ionie said.

"I don't know – but we did it!" said Maia, getting to her feet and looking at the ground where the Shade had been. "We sent it back to the Shadows."

Bracken and Juniper raced round in happy circles. Willow bucked and even Sorrel gave a satisfied meow. "Well done, everyone!" she declared.

"The shed!" exclaimed Sita, looking round and seeing that the branches of the bonfire were burning merrily and that the flames were starting to lick at the wooden sides of the shed. "We have to put out the fire!"

The girls grabbed buckets from inside the shed and with Lottie running at top speed back and forth between the shed and the large water butt full of rainwater, they emptied bucket after bucket over the flames.

The fire was finally extinguished, leaving the air heavy with the smell of smoke. The shed, thankfully, was unharmed apart from a few scorch marks round the back.

The girls collapsed on the ground, hugging their animals.

"We fought another Shade," said Maia.

"What do you think he meant," said Ionie, "when he said all that stuff about one of us having lots of power?"

"You must be the one the Shade spoke of, Ionie," said Sorrel.

"It said the person who conjured the Shade is a she," said Bracken.

"We need to find her, whoever she is, and stop her," said Juniper.

"Let's worry about that another day," said Lottie. "I've had enough excitement for now. I just want to go and have a sleepover!"

"Me, too," said Ionie, with a smile.

Maia got to her feet. "We'd better say goodbye to Paige."

Ionie nodded and she and Maia headed back to the house. Paige was still watching the music awards with Clio.

"I thought you'd gone home," said Clio in surprise.

"We're just off now," said Maia. "The gnome's gone, Paige."

"Gone? For good?" said Paige eagerly.

Maia and Ionie nodded.

"You mean that cute little pottery gnome?" said Clio. "What's happened to it?"

"It smashed," said Maia.

"Maia! What will Paige's mum and dad say?" Clio said anxiously.

"Don't worry – they didn't really like it," said Paige. "I think they'll be glad it's gone." She smiled at Maia and Ionie in relief.

"Thanks!"

"No problem. See you soon." Ionie and Maia waved and left.

As they walked round the house to join the others, Maia glanced at Ionie. She couldn't help thinking about what the gnome had said when she had been locked in the shed with Lottie and Sita. Surely Ionie wasn't really jealous of her, was she?

Ionie saw her glance. "What?" she said warily.

"The gnome said some stuff when I was in the shed. You're not really jealous of me, are you?"

Ionie's cheeks flushed bright red. "No," she said, avoiding Maia's gaze. "Course not."

Maia's eyes widened. Ionie's blush gave her away even though she was denying it. But why? She was so clever.

"So what if you're popular and everyone likes you," Ionie went on defensively. "That's you. I'm me. I'm fine with it."

Maia didn't know what to say. She swallowed. "Oh. OK. Well, just so you know … I'm … I'm glad you became a Star Friend, too." The words came out in a rush. Her mind flashed back to being in the house with Ionie and Sorrel, tracking down the gnome, and she realized she meant it. "Thank you for helping me with my magic. That stuff you said about relaxing really worked and … well, it's been fun doing stuff together today."

Their eyes met. Ionie's face softened. "It has been, hasn't it? We make a good team. Bracken and Sorrel do, too – only don't tell Sorrel I said that," she added.

"No way," said Maia. "I wouldn't dare."

They exchanged grins and carried on in silence. Maia's steps felt suddenly lighter. Maybe she and Ionie could be friends again after all – proper friends.

Lottie and Sita were waiting for them by the trampoline. Maia held up her hand and they high-fived her. "We did it," she said. "We sent another Shade back to the Shadows."

Lottie linked arms with her. "It's sleepover time."

"Time to toast marshmallows on the bonfire," said Ionie.

"And eat cinder toffee," said Maia.

"And no need to worry about fighting any more Shades tonight," added Sita happily.

A couple of hours later, they were all snuggled down in Maia's room with their animals lying beside them or cuddled in their arms. They were full of marshmallows and sweets.

"It's been such a scary few days." Sita sighed. "I'm glad it's over and no one else is going to get hurt."

"For now," said Sorrel darkly. "The person who trapped the Shade is still out there somewhere. We should be looking for her."

Bracken made a grumbling noise in his throat. "One night off isn't going to hurt us."

Sorrel looked at him dryly. "It's not us I'm worried about."

Ionie stroked her. "It's all right, Sorrel. We'll start trying to find the person who conjured the Shade tomorrow."

"I wonder if Paige's family were given the gnome on purpose," Sita said.

They were all silent for a moment. It was horrible to think of someone deliberately setting out to bring misery to Paige or her family.

"Whoever trapped the Shade must be really evil," said Lottie with a shiver.

"But one of us is more powerful," Ionie reminded them. "That's what the Shade said."

"I'm sure it's you," purred Sorrel. "After all, you're the Spirit Speaker."

"I think it's Maia," said Bracken loyally. "Her magic is getting stronger all the time. Soon she'll be able to look into the past and even see into people's thoughts."

"Useful, I agree," said Sorrel. "But she's not as powerful as Ionie."

"It could be Lottie," put in Juniper, snuggling his head under Lottie's chin.

"Yep, with my deadly apple-throwing ability," said Lottie with a grin.

"As long as it's not me," said Sita. "I don't want to be powerful. I just want to heal people and make them better."

Maia thought about it. She liked the thought of being really powerful and being able to scare people who were using dark magic. Which of them would it be? As she considered it, a wave of tiredness suddenly swept over her and she yawned. "Shall we turn off the light?"

The others all nodded sleepily.

"Night, everyone," Maia whispered.

"Night," came the sighs back.

Bracken snuggled down on Maia's chest and licked the tip of her nose. She smiled and kissed the soft spot between his ears. She felt safe and warm and happy. She was surrounded by her best friends with Bracken by her side. There was no doubt they were going to have more excitement but for now fighting evil and doing magic could wait until another day.

"Night, Bracken," she whispered into his ear.

Snuffling contentedly, he snuggled closer into her arms.

HAVE YOU READ?

StarFriends

MIRROR MAGIC

LINDA CHAPMAN

ILLUSTRATED BY LUCY FLEMING

DO YOU BELIEVE IN MAGIC?

Maia and her friends do! And when they meet the Star Animals, a whole world of magical adventure unfolds.

Maia's older sister has started acting strangely and the Star Animals sense dark magic at work. Can the girls use their newfound Star Magic to help them put a stop to it?

About the Author

Linda Chapman is the best-selling author of over 200 books. The biggest compliment Linda can have is for a child to tell her they became a reader after reading one of her books. Linda lives in a cottage with a tower in Leicestershire with her husband, three children, three dogs and three ponies. When she's not writing, Linda likes to ride, read and visit schools and libraries to talk to people about writing.

www.lindachapmanauthor.co.uk

About the Illustrator

Lucy Fleming has been an avid doodler and bookworm since early childhood. Drawing always seemed like so much fun but she never dreamed it could be a full-time job! She lives and works in a small town in England with her partner and a little black cat. When not at her desk she likes nothing more than to be outdoors in the sunshine with a hot cup of tea.

www.lucyflemingillustrations.com